CU0024I109

All Change

For my mum, Mary Carrington, who always believed in me; for my children, Joe, Laurey and Dan, who were my guinea pigs; for my grandchildren Rio, Millie, Sonny and Amalie; and for all the children in the classes I taught, who listened and laughed at the seeds of this story.

ALL CHANGE

Chapter 1   **Swimming again?**

"Mrs Peacock said to bring our swimming stuff tomorrow," Ben said to his mum at teatime. It was odd. They never went swimming on Fridays.

"*Tomorrow*?" Ben's mum stopped wiping pasta sauce from baby Ella's face and turned to face Ben. "Tomorrow's Friday."

"I *know* it's Friday." he replied, raising his fork carefully to his mouth, and giving his mum an exasperated look. "Just as we were putting our chairs up she shouted out *don't forget your swimming things tomorrow*. I know

4

that's what she said 'cos Jake asked why."

"It's just a bit strange, that's all," said Ben's mum, "swimming's *always* been on Wednesdays. You've been this week." Ben's mum pulled the pasta-stained bib over Ella's head in one practised move, "What did she say to Jake?"

"She told Jake off for shouting out," said Ben. He watched as sauce dripped from his fork onto the table, "then she just said we'd have to wait and see. We'll find out tomorrow." Ben's mum sighed, "She's nutty as a fruitcake," she muttered as she lifted a wriggling Ella from her highchair.

5

Ben frowned. He thought Mrs Peacock was brilliant. She let them eat their fruit on the playground, not inside like other classes; she didn't bother too much if they couldn't line up in alphabetical order, even after two terms; and she let them go early for lunch if they weren't silly at milk time (admittedly that wasn't often). Best of all, she told the most fantastic stories – all about magic conkers that granted wishes, and carrots with legs that could run across the playground. And the puppets in Mrs Peacock's classroom came to life at night. Ben knew that because Mrs Peacock showed them the banana skins and sweet wrappers left on the floor.

Just lately though, she did *shout* rather a lot, and her face was nearly always bright red, even *before* school started these days, and her hair was beginning to look a bit like the hair on that doll of Ella's – all matted and sticking up in funny places. Anyway, none of that really mattered to Ben. The stories were much more important.

"Got your trunks?" asked Jake excitedly, as he answered the door to Ben the following morning.

"Yeah," Ben grinned, feeling the weight of the rolled towel in his backpack, and gave a secret shiver of anticipation

"Hey, I wonder what time we'll go," Jake looked eagerly across at Ben, awaiting an answer. Ben knew everything. Ben knew the names of all the planets. In order. Ben knew his five times table, even nine fives. Ben knew that you *never* started a sentence with "and". And Ben knew that mustard and cress needed water *and* light (Jake had confidently said just water and then watched worriedly as Mrs Peacock put his damp, seedy flannel into the dark art cupboard. He'd been so disappointed when Mrs Peacock had produced the brown shrivelled stems from the cupboard a few days later, although she had seemed delighted – she said it proved a hypothesis – whatever that might mean. He had forgotten to ask Ben later.)

"We might miss Circle Time," said Ben excitedly. Up until last week he'd always liked Circle Time. You got to talk about your feelings and everybody had to listen. Nobody was allowed to laugh, whatever you said. You had to wait to speak and it was only your turn when you were passed the wooden cow that Mrs Peacock's daughter had brought her back from Yarmouth one holiday. Those were the rules. Ben liked rules. You knew where you were with them.

That's what his mum said. Mrs Peacock said it was a pity that there was always somebody who had to break the rules and spoil it.

And that's what had happened last week. Joe Rimmer had broken the rules and spoiled it. Just as Ben had been telling everyone, in a very serious voice, how it made him feel when his baby sister was born, and Mrs Peacock was looking at him with her head on one side, nodding in a kindly sort of way, Joe Rimmer had shouted out something about babies' pooey nappies, and everybody had burst out laughing so loud that Ben's serious voice could no longer be heard. Ben had felt like crying. It made him feel slightly better to see Joe sitting on the naughty chair, and Mrs Peacock leaning across him, prodding at the air with her finger as everyone else went out to play, but he knew Joe wouldn't really care. Ben hated Circle Time now. It reminded him of the day that Joe Rimmer broke the rules and spoiled it for him.

"Oh yeah, that would be good – swimming instead of Circle Time," Jake laughed. He had always hated Circle Time. He never knew what to say when he found himself holding the wooden cow, warm and sticky from the fingers of the other children.

"S'funny going twice in one week though," Ben was saying to the group of boys, leaning against the wall in the playground. There was a large, untidy pile of bags by their feet. Towels and goggles spilled onto the ground, and into nearby puddles.

"She did say it was the only time we were quiet," said Matty, scuffing his shoe against the wall, "when we were in the pool. Still don't know why we're going again though."

"Well," shouted Jake, as Matty's voice was drowned out by the sound of a loud

whistle, "won't be long before we find
out."

Chapter 2   <u>**Strange Instructions**</u>

Mrs Peacock stood facing the playground, "Come on 4P, line up sensibly!" she was shouting, her eyes darting backwards and forwards, like a giant lizard's. She looked as though she knew nobody was listening. All around her children were pushing, shoving, shouting and yelling, and finally lining up in front of their teachers. Mrs Peacock's line contained one child. Kimberley had been pushed to the line in her wheelchair, and was waiting patiently for the rest of the class.

Ben glanced across. "C'mon,

Jake," he called, grabbing his friend's arm and throwing his backpack over his shoulder. They raced to the line. Mrs Peacock had once told the children she wished she had a large well-trained sheepdog to round them all up and herd them into school. The children had rolled on the floor, nudging each other and laughing so much that Leah Morgan had been taken straight to the toilets by Mrs Barlow, the class helper, and had come back looking embarrassed, clutching a carrier bag. Ben had joined in with the laughter, but now, looking at Mrs Peacock's face, he began to wonder if she hadn't meant it to be funny. Maybe she was being serious.

He felt sorry for her. It must be hard work being a teacher, especially when nobody did as they were told, and everybody was so noisy all the time, and you had to stay in with somebody (usually Joe Rimmer) every playtime, so you didn't even get the caffeine fix (whatever that was) that Mrs Peacock was always telling Mrs Barlow she needed.

From his place in the line behind Jake, Ben glanced back. He hoped the other children would hurry up. He sneaked a look at Mrs Peacock's face from behind Jake's rucksack. Strangely, her expression had changed. She looked – Ben struggled to think how to describe it – she looked *excited.* He felt puzzled. He had only ever seen children look excited before, not adults, and certainly not teachers. Paul Matthews ran across the playground, his swimming towel trailing on the ground behind him. Using Leah as a buffer he came to a halt at the end of the line, and gathered his towel in a messy bundle under his arm. The playground was empty now, no strays. The other classes had all gone in.

Ben looked at Mrs Peacock expectantly. This was usually when she told the children how disappointed she was with them. How, once again, they were the last class to line up. But Mrs Peacock still had that odd, excited look on her face. She blew one long blast of her whistle in the short pause that followed, and said in a loud voice, that sounded a bit wobbly and strange to Ben, "*Right*, children - " Jake turned round to Ben and made a face like a monkey. Ben would have laughed at this on a normal day, but today evidently wasn't a normal day. It was definitely a *not normal* day. A *very not normal* day.

Ben ignored Jake and continued to stare at Mrs Peacock, who was still talking in that loud, wobbly voice, "...so, it's a change of plan today…" Ben could hear Danny whistling through the gap in his teeth. He knew Danny would be getting excited at the thought of a *change of plan*. That sounded fun. Mrs Peacock frowned at Danny, "We are going to go round the side of the building, outside the classroom window".

Danny whistled again. Ben felt his tummy flip. If Danny whistled one more time Mrs Peacock might not carry out her change of plan. She might decide to have a normal Friday morning with Literacy and Numeracy and Circle Time. Mrs Peacock stopped talking and stared hard at Danny. Ben held his breath. Danny closed his mouth and looked down at his feet. Mrs Peacock continued, "When we get round there you will all change out of your school uniforms and into your swimwear." Danny's whistle could not be heard above the loud cheer that came from the rest of the class.

Ben felt stunned. What was Mrs Peacock talking about? They never got changed *outside*, they did that in the classroom. In the warm. Jake nudged Ben, "We've got to take off our clothes *in the playground*?" he hissed, as if he couldn't believe it. Ben nodded, feeling sick.

"No way!" said Jake, screwing up his face.

Chapter 3   <u>Locked in</u>

The line of children snaked noisily around the corner of the building and along one side. Mrs Peacock led the way, her whistle swinging on a length of green string round her neck. Ben couldn't understand why nobody was asking any questions. Joe Rimmer - why wasn't he shouting out? Ben looked behind him and saw Joe laughing with Nathan. They were both taking giant strides, catching the heels of the children in front with each step. Nobody else seemed to think it was funny that Mrs Peacock had said they were going to get changed outside. Or perhaps they were just so excited that there was a *change of plan* that they didn't want to remind Mrs Peacock that this was not a normal day.

Mrs Peacock stopped by the classroom window and turned to face the children. She blew the whistle once, so quietly that Ben thought it was Danny, through that gap in his teeth. "Children," said Mrs Peacock, and Ben noticed that strange excited look again, "get yourselves changed as quickly as possible, leave the towels in your bags and put your bags behind this drainpipe. Look - " she grabbed a bag, screwed it up as tightly as she could and pushed it behind the drainpipe, "You see," she said, "or rather you don't see - " She began to laugh loudly, a bit madly, Ben thought, like the monster in his reading book, that couldn't stop laughing and ended up exploding with a huge bang. Ben felt a strange worrying feeling building up in his tummy. He was beginning to wish it was a normal day and he was doing Circle Time.

"Right, I need a monitor," said Mrs Peacock, when she had stopped laughing. Ben was relieved that she hadn't exploded. His hand shot up in the air and he stood on tiptoe. Mrs Peacock looked at the sea of stiffly waving hands and beckoned to Ben. He walked proudly past Jake and Abby and Joe and Kimberley, and stood looking up at Mrs Peacock. She bent to whisper in his ear, "I want you to go into school, walk *quietly* up to Mrs Craven's office and close her door. Turn the key in the lock. *Don't* let her see you." Ben stared at Mrs Peacock. She was staring back at him. He swallowed and nodded. He could tell this was a really important job. He wanted to do it but he was a bit worried about doing it on his own. Mrs Craven was the Headteacher. You didn't lock the Headteacher in her room. What if she saw him before he could turn the key? What if she wasn't in her office but outside it, telling off that horrible Ryan, who was always in trouble.

"Can I take someone with me?" he whispered, but Mrs Peacock had already turned away and was trying to pull Abby's swimming cap onto her head. For once, Ben was glad that Jake never did as he was told, at least first time. Jake was still in his school uniform, chatting to Joe. They were swinging their trunks round above their heads and making silly monkey faces. "Jake," hissed Ben, "come on, we've got an important job to do." Jake didn't usually get important jobs. He wasn't to be trusted, Mrs Peacock said. The two boys left their swimming things by the wall and walked importantly towards the front entrance of the school. Ben was beginning to enjoy this now. Mrs Peacock might be nutty as a fruitcake but this was better than Literacy.

Ben turned to face Jake and put his finger to his lips, then he bent over and began to tiptoe up the corridor. Jake immediately followed, two paces behind. This was fun. It was like playing army where you had to sneak up on the enemy. As Ben approached the office, he lowered his head like some sort of strange beast, so that Mrs Brookes, the school clerk wouldn't see him through the hatch. He could hear the tap tap of her keyboard as he crept along, close to the wall. He could feel Jake's breath on the back of his neck, and for the second time that morning he shivered with excitement. Ben and Jake had lowered themselves onto their bellies by the time they reached the door to Mrs Craven's office. They were soldiers, on manoeuvres, Ben said. Jake wasn't sure what that meant, but it sounded good.

The door was open slightly, and Jake could hear Mrs Craven on the phone. "Yes," she was saying, "I understand that, Mrs Peters, but Ryan really can't go round doing these things to other children. There have to be consequences." Ben didn't know what consequences were but they sounded bad. He hoped they were. He eased himself up off the floor, making sure he remained behind the door. Jake did the same. The two boys looked at each other and grinned. Ben reached across and clutched the key sticking out of the lock. It was smooth and cool against his palm. He heard the ping of the 'phone as Mrs Craven replaced the receiver. In one swift move, Ben pushed the door closed and turned the key firmly in the lock until he heard a satisfying click.

Chapter 4   <u>All Change</u>

By the time Ben and Jake had sneaked down the corridor and arrived back by the classroom window most of the children were changed into their swimming things. Joe Rimmer was prancing up and down in his underpants, acting like a ballerina, but that was no surprise, thought Ben. Four girls in swimsuits and hats were huddled together by the wall, knees bent, shivering and giggling at Joe. Amy's white hat was pulled down so tight and low over her eyebrows that her head reminded Ben of a boiled egg. He grinned to himself and kicked off his shoes. Good job his mum couldn't see those laces still tied. He was a bit worried about getting undressed in front of everyone, especially Megan, who said she was his girlfriend. He certainly didn't want her catching sight of the Batman undies he was wearing. They had a label in them saying age 4 – 6. His mum kept saying *they'd do*. Only now, out on the cold playground, he knew they most certainly would *not do*.

He twisted his head round and searched the group for Jake. Oh, good idea! Jake had wrapped his towel around his waist and was bent double, wriggling into his trunks. His boxers floated in a puddle by the drainpipe. Ben took the towel out of his backpack and quickly wound it round himself. He'd be ready before he knew it, as his grandma would say.

"Oi, Joe, are you the Sugar Plum Fairy?" laughed Matty. Joe stopped twirling round and tried to stand up straight. It was impossible. He began to fall to one side, crashed into Abby and bounced back the other way. "Ouch!" shouted Abby, rubbing her arm. Ben slipped one leg into his trunks and balanced on the other foot, holding onto the wall for support. What happened next was just like one of those cartoons you see on the telly. That's what Ben thought afterwards. At the time, he didn't think anything.

It was bad luck for Leah that she bent over to pick up her swimming bag at the very moment Joe was bouncing back off Abby's arm. Joe did a funny little one-legged half turn and fell sideways onto Leah's swimsuited bottom. The force of Joe's weight shunted Leah into the most energetic forward roll she had ever performed. It was also bad luck, Ben decided later, that he was still balancing on one foot when Leah crashed into his other leg – the one that was waving about in midair, with a pair of swimming trunks hanging from the ankle. Ben felt himself falling backwards. Desperately, one hand clutched at his towel. If it fell off now it would be even worse than everyone seeing his Batman undies. As he went down, his other hand clutched at the air around him, trying to find something - anything - to grab hold of and stop himself hitting the ground. He closed his eyes. His hand, palm outwards, came up against something soft. He grabbed it. Ben opened his eyes and tried to focus. He looked towards his hand. To his horror, he was hanging on to Mrs Peacock's leg.

Mrs Peacock looked down at her

leg, and at the hand attached to it. She shook her leg vigorously, as if to remove an insect. Ben released his grip and let his hand fall, with the rest of him, to the ground. He looked up. Mrs Peacock was wearing a swirly pink and purple swimming costume and a hat with plastic flowers that waved as she moved. From Ben's position on the ground she looked enormous. A crowd of children had gathered round them. It was like a circus, thought Ben, with him and Leah and Amy and Joe the performers. Mrs Peacock must be the Ringmaster. Ben picked himself up, making sure he hung onto his towel. "Right," said Mrs Peacock, still in that wobbly voice. The flowers on her hat shivered as she spoke, "everybody line up by the drainpipe. We're ready for the next step." Danny whistled.

Ben and Joe pulled on their trunks and threw their towels behind the drainpipe. The children shuffled into place and looked at Mrs Peacock, waiting for the next instruction. Mrs Peacock cast her eyes quickly over their faces. She must need somebody very sensible, thought Ben, that's what she does before she chooses someone for an important job. He straightened his back and looked earnestly up at her.

"Ben," said Mrs Peacock, after a few

36

seconds, "see that hosepipe - " Ben's eyes followed the line of Mrs Peacock's pointing finger. He hadn't noticed it before, but now he could see the hosepipe attached to the outside tap. It ran up the wall by the drainpipe and disappeared onto the roof. Ben wondered where it went after that. "I want you to climb up the drainpipe - " Danny whistled long and loud, and Joe Rimmer shouted out, "Apeman!". Mrs Peacock carried on as if she hadn't heard them. Her eyes looked really strange now, " - follow the hosepipe to the nozzle at the end. Then wait for the rest of us there."

Chapter 5   In at the Deep End

Ben lay on his tummy across the roof, his feet wedged against the rough tiles, and peered down through the open skylight window into the classroom. He blinked. He couldn't believe his eyes. Mrs Peacock had told Ben to follow the hosepipe to the nozzle at the end. He had followed the hosepipe up the wall and onto the roof, over the roof and now, as he stopped at the skylight, he could see the nozzle at the end of the hosepipe, hanging down into the classroom, dangling just above – Ben blinked again and opened his eyes wide – just above the water. The water came up to the top of the really high cupboards, the ones nobody could reach without a ladder, even Mr McCann, the caretaker, who was like a giant.

Ben squinted through the open skylight. He couldn't see anything that was usually in the classroom, like tables or chairs or the sticker charts or the Star of the Week board. He couldn't see the display board with his poem about Autumn. He felt a bit sad about that. It had taken him ages trying to find a word that rhymed with conkers. His mum said bonkers wasn't really appropriate, and plonkers was just downright rude, which meant he couldn't use them. In the end he had changed it to nuts instead. Ben focused his eyes on the tops of the tall cupboards. That was strange. The pencil pots were lined up against the wall, next to the ruler drawer, which had been removed from a unit above three other drawers. These drawers were also on top of the cupboards. He could see the labels from here: scrap paper; felt tip pens; crayons. Exercise books were piled, in untidy heaps, next to the ruler drawer – Literacy, Numeracy, RE, Science, and one he didn't recognise, probably History. They hadn't done that this year. Mrs Peacock had said history would start in the summer term. Ben's mum and dad had laughed when he'd told them, although Ben had no idea why. He could see the poster of a Roman soldier, poking out of the top cupboard, ready for the summer term.

Propped up against the exercise books was the register, with a pen clipped to the top, and next to that, a box of fruit – apples again, thought Ben with a sigh. The tray of class milk was balanced, at a dangerous angle, on top of some of the exercise books. Ben hoped the cartons wouldn't start to slide down into the water. At least, not until Mrs Peacock arrived, and then it wouldn't be his fault. It looked to Ben as if Mrs Peacock had put all those things on top of the cupboard to keep them dry. She must have planned all this, thought Ben, in amazement. That must have been what she meant when she said there was a change of plan.

"Ben?!"

Ben jumped and sat up. "Have you got to the nozzle yet?" Mrs Peacock's voice sounded close even though she was still on the ground. Ben had been so busy looking in amazement at his classroom that he'd forgotten about Mrs Peacock and the other children. "Just found it," Ben called back. He could hear his friends, down by the drainpipe.

"Where is he?"

"What's he doing?"

"Wish he'd hurry up,"

"Can we go up there Miss?"

"What's happening?"

"I'm freezing,"

"SSSSSSSHHHHHHH!" That was Mrs Peacock. It was the longest SSSHHH that Ben had ever heard. Everything went quiet.

"What shall I do?" shouted Ben, hoping that Mrs Peacock would be quick to tell him. He was getting cold and his feet were beginning to slip on the tiles. "Hang on to the hosepipe," hissed Mrs Peacock, "and drop down."

Ben heard Danny whistle. He knew Mrs Peacock would be giving him one of her looks – the one that made you suddenly stare down at your own feet.

"Hold tight to the nozzle!" added Mrs Peacock, in a shrill voice, but Ben had already swung his legs down through the skylight and was hanging by the hosepipe only centimetres from the water. Slowly he let his hands slide down the pipe. His toes touched the water. It was cold, but not unbearable. He slid down a bit further. His legs followed his toes and his feet. The water was up to the bottom of his trunks. He wondered whether the radiators were on. They would heat the water a bit. He took a deep breath and let his hands slide down the hosepipe as far as they could go. When they reached the nozzle they stopped. Ben's body was right under the water. His arms reached up to the hosepipe. Only his head bobbed above the surface.

Chapter 6   <u>**Dropping in**</u>

Ben clung to the hosepipe as if his life depended on it. He knew he didn't need it to keep afloat. He could swim, even in his pyjamas, he could go down to the bottom and pick up a coin, and he could do a star float for a whole minute. No, he hung on to the hosepipe because Mrs Peacock had told him to. He always did as he was told by teachers. He didn't like to think about what might happen if he didn't. The hosepipe suddenly jerked and began to rise in the air. Ben found himself being sucked up out of the water.

"*Hey!*" he yelled, wriggling like a fish on

the end of a fishing line, *"What's going on?!"* The hosepipe stopped moving. He heard Mrs Peacock's voice from down below again, *"Leah, let go of the hosepipe, just hang onto the roof tiles."* The hosepipe dropped down into the classroom, taking Ben with it. He plopped back down into the water. He could feel himself going under and hoped he wouldn't go right to the bottom. He knew it would be a long way, and he might never come up again. He tightened his grip on the hosepipe and bounced back up like a yoyo. He emerged from the water, gasping for breath, spluttering, and rubbing at his face with one hand. With the other he still clung to the hosepipe.

When Ben opened his eyes it took him a moment to focus. He was surprised to see Leah bobbing about beside him. They looked at each other, and Ben grinned.

"What's going on?" he asked, but Leah shook her head and coughed loudly. She looked as if she had just swallowed a large amount of water. Just as she opened her mouth to speak there was a loud splash and something disappeared beneath the surface of the water. Ben and Leah were swept backwards, frantically paddling with their feet. Ben knocked his head on the cupboard door and two cartons of milk tumbled down into the water. A head bobbed into view, eyes and mouth tightly closed. It was Jake.

"Mrs Peacock's sending us all up," spluttered Jake, opening his eyes and turning his head to look at Ben, "one at a time." A pair of feet appeared above them, quickly followed by the rest of the body. Joe Rimmer slid down the hosepipe and crashed into Ben, sending him flying to the side. Ben's arms flailed wildly. He crashed headlong into the cupboard and another avalanche of milk toppled down. Ben disappeared under the water, taking the hosepipe with him, as the others ducked and shielded their faces with their arms. Joe Rimmer spoiling things again, thought Ben, angrily, as he came up for air. There was another loud splash, and Ben, Leah, Jake and Joe rose and fell, crashing into each other like boats battered by a rough sea.

"Whhhooooaaaahhh!" shouted Jake, grabbing at Ben's arm.

By the time twenty-five more children had dropped in through the skylight and were bobbing about in the water, Ben was feeling rather seasick. He was certainly sick of being flung about in the water every time another child splashed down. He was still hanging onto the hosepipe, but he wished now he hadn't been given that important job. He would rather be swimming around like Nathan and Amy or messing about with Jake. He glanced across the classroom. Jake and Joe Rimmer were diving down into the water and swimming between each other's legs. They kept bursting out of the water and laughing.

Suddenly the room went dark. Somebody warbled, "Ooooohhhhh," in a ghostly voice and everybody laughed. Danny whistled. Ben tipped his head back into the water and looked up. Above him dangled a pair of very podgy,

51

rather old looking feet, and, completely blocking the skylight, was Mrs Peacock's large, swirly pink and purple bottom. Ben gasped. He'd never seen such a huge bottom at close quarters. Mrs Peacock's bottom never looked as big as that when she had her brown skirt on. Nobody spoke. All eyes were on Mrs Peacock's bottom.

"Mind out of the way, children!" shouted Mrs Peacock in a shrill voice, "I'm coming iiiiiiiiinnnnnnnnnnn!"

The last word was drowned out as Mrs Peacock dropped like a lead weight through the skylight, and disappeared with a loud splash under the water. Large ripples began to spread across the surface, gaining momentum until waves splashed up the walls, and the Roman soldier floated across the room.

"Wow!" yelled Joe Rimmer, "It's like the wave machine at Water World!" Jake opened his mouth to laugh and took a large gulp of water. Ben could see his friends, all around him, rising up with the swell, and plummeting down again as the waves subsided. He glanced at Mrs Peacock, who had bounced to the surface, coughing and spluttering. The flowers on her cap shook alarmingly. She didn't look as though she had heard Joe Rimmer. If she had she'd have told him to go outside the room, thought Ben, before realising that this would be impossible today. He giggled to himself and, still clutching the hosepipe, swam determinedly towards the shivering flowers.

Chapter 7   <u>**Down to Work**</u>

Ben could see Mrs Peacock's legs, moving frantically beneath the surface of the water. Her arms made strange doggy paddle movements, like Ella's when his mum took them swimming. "Everybody, tread water," said Mrs Peacock. She sounded out of breath, as though speaking was a real effort, "just move your legs up and down as if- ," she ran out of breath and paused for a second, " – as if you're pedalling a bike." The water began to bubble like a huge stew, as thirty pairs of legs began pedalling madly, and arms thrashed about on the surface. Seven more cartons of milk splashed into the water. The eighth bounced off Matty's shoulder, skimmed Abby's arm and flew through the air. Ben watched as the milk made its way across the room and rebounded off the cupboard door. Even before it happened, he knew with absolute certainty that it was going to land on Mrs Peacock's head. Ben's mouth hung open. His eyes were wide. He forgot to tread water. Just as he sank beneath the surface, Ben saw the carton smack into the side of Mrs Peacock's head. The last thing he remembered before totally submerging was the carton bursting with a bang and milk spraying over the plastic flowers, like water from a watering can.

It seemed to Ben a very long time before he came bobbing back up to the surface. Mrs Peacock was still doing that strange doggy paddle thing with one hand, but the other hand was wiping at her face, spreading milk across it just like Ella did. Each time she moved her head the flowers shook and milk scattered through the air. Finally, Mrs Peacock gave one huge shake of her head, like a dog getting out of a pond, and the last drops of milk flew out all around her. Joe Rimmer licked his lips and raised his eyebrows, as if this was the best drink he had ever tasted. Ben pulled a face. Trust Joe Rimmer to think it was nice.

"It's not milk time yet," said Mrs Peacock. Somebody sniggered. Ben thought it was probably Joe Rimmer, but he couldn't be certain. "We have work to do," she continued, glancing up at the books on top of the cupboard. The children looked at each other in amazement. How were they supposed to do their work *in the water?* More to the point, *why* were they doing their work in the water?

"Miss," said Jake, glancing across at Ben with a puzzled expression, "why have you filled the classroom with water?" Mrs Peacock paused from reaching out to the top of the cupboard, and turned to face Jake. "Because," she said, slowly and seriously, "I noticed that the only time this class was quiet was when I took you swimming. As soon as you all got in the water it was lovely." She closed her eyes and smiled, "Total silence." Ben nodded. It was all beginning to make sense. Mrs Peacock had grabbed the top of the cupboard and was trying to heave herself out of the water. Her feet scrabbled against the door, trying to get a grip. Her body rose up and dropped back into the water as her feet slid down the door.

Ben felt sorry for her. She looked like that fat beetle he had caught once, and trapped in a jam jar. It had spent the whole afternoon trying to escape, climbing up the side of the jar, getting nearly to the top and then sliding back down again. In the end Ben had taken pity on it and tipped it out in the garden. Mrs Peacock wasn't going to be quite so easy to deal with. Ben took hold of Jake's arm and dragged him towards Mrs Peacock. She had managed to get her feet a bit higher and was in a hunched position, wobbling dangerously above the water. From where Ben was he couldn't see Mrs Peacock's face. Her big swirly pink and purple bottom was in the way.

"Mrs Peacock!" shouted Ben to the bottom, "We'll help you, me and Jake. Stand on our shoulders."

The scrabbling stopped and one foot felt its way slowly onto Ben's shoulder. Ben was surprised at how heavy it was. His shoulder sank down into the water, and he grabbed at an arm beside him. He turned his head to see Joe Rimmer. "Help us, Joe," he said, feeling annoyed that it was Joe Rimmer. He hoped he wouldn't spoil things again. "Hang on to me and Jake, then if someone can hang onto you - " Matty clutched at Joe's shoulder, and before Ben knew it, everybody was hanging onto somebody, and Mrs Peacock was balancing one foot on Ben's shoulder and one foot on Jake's. The water swirled and splashed as the giant web of children spread across the water.

Mrs Peacock stretched her arms up and reached for a pile of books. Her body shook. Ben and Jake shook. Joe Rimmer shook. Matty shook. The shaking spread across the web, so that it wobbled like an unset jelly. Mrs Peacock grabbed the books and held them tight to her chest with one arm. Ben wished she would hurry up now.

His shoulder was hurting and he had swallowed a lot of water. He looked up, keeping his head as still as he could.

"Just the pencils now," said Mrs Peacock, in that excited voice again, reaching out with her spare hand, "then we'll be all set." She was practically balancing on her left foot now, as she leaned across to the back of the cupboard. Ben was glad it was Jake's shoulder under that foot, and not his.

At that moment there was a loud knocking at the door. Mrs Peacock's right foot dropped back down onto Ben's shoulder with a thump. Everybody was suddenly very still, as though it was a game of water statues and the music had just stopped. The only noise was the lapping of the water against the walls, and Ben's heart beating in his chest.

Chapter 8   <u>**Flood**</u>

All eyes were on Mrs Peacock.
She blinked hard three times and
twisted her head towards the door.
Through the frosted glass she saw the
outline of an adult, an adult who looked
suspiciously like Mrs Craven.

"Who – who is it?" called Mrs Peacock,
trying to sound as though she was
sitting at her desk, marking books.

"It's Mrs Craven!" shouted the outline.
She didn't sound very happy. Ben didn't
feel very happy. He had locked her in
her room and now she had escaped.
What could he say? She would never
believe Mrs Peacock had told him to do

it. And it was no use asking Jake to back him up. Mrs Peacock said Jake never knew what day it was. There was no way he would know what Mrs Peacock had asked him to do. Ben began to shiver, although his face felt strangely hot. It was that horrible panicky feeling he had when Mrs Peacock asked him a question he couldn't answer. It always happened when he hadn't been listening for a minute, and everybody seemed to be waiting for him.

The banging on the door started up again, only louder this time. Much louder. An angry sort of knock, thought

Ben worriedly. What would Mrs Craven do to him when she found out he was the one who had locked her in? He couldn't bear to think about it. Nobody spoke. Everybody continued to stare at Mrs Peacock. Teachers always knew what to do. Mrs Peacock took a deep breath and looked as though she was about to shout, "just a minute!" or, "hang on there!" in that high wobbly voice that she'd been using today, when a loud squeaking noise rose up through the water. Ben looked towards the noise. Three milk cartons floated by, in single file, like barges on a canal. He could see Leah's and Megan's and Joe's and Mattie's legs pumping up and down without a sound, he could see the outline of Mrs Craven's head through the glass, and with horror he realised he could see the door knob turning very, very slowly. Mrs Craven's head had disappeared from view. Ben guessed she was crouching down, concentrating on the door knob, trying to turn it with two hands. Mrs Peacock was staring at the door as though she had never seen it before. She didn't speak but the flowers on her hat trembled worryingly.

Ben decided there was only one thing to do. He took a deep breath, turned himself around, thrust his head under the water and paddled desperately with his legs until he was completely upside down. Then he headed for the door. Ben grabbed the door knob. He felt it spin through his hands. It had turned nearly enough for the door to open. With all his might Ben turned the door knob in the opposite direction. It turned back again. Ben could hardly breathe. He needed air. There was a loud click. Ben felt the doorknob slipping out of his grasp. The door flew open and water began to gush out of the room, carrying Ben with it. This was even more like Water World – like the big chute that carried you, tossing and turning, all the way from the top of the building down into the swirling water. Ben's eyes were tight shut. He gasped and gulped, swept along like a fish in the tide. He had been so startled to be flying down the corridor like this that he hadn't noticed the screaming noise which seemed to be following him. "Aaaaaaaarrrrrrgggggghhhhhh! Aaaaaaaaaarrrrrrrggggggghhhhhhh!"

It was getting louder and nearer to him. With a huge effort, Ben turned his head and looked behind him. A large sea monster was hurtling towards him on the crest of a wave. Ben was terrified. It might eat him. He looked again, and drew in his breath. He could not believe his eyes. It was Mrs Craven, on her back, arms and legs waving in the air. That was even more scary than a sea monster. If Mrs Craven caught up, he didn't like to think what she might do to him. She certainly looked – and sounded – very angry now. Ben turned away from Mrs Craven and looked ahead, down the corridor. He could see Mr McCann on a step ladder in the distance, wobbling slightly, reaching up to a dangling light bulb, unaware of the water racing towards him. Ben thrashed his legs up and down as though his life depended on it. Which, he thought worriedly, it might well do if Mrs Craven had anything to do with it. His arms felt like rubber. They seemed to be moving about, waving and slicing through the water, without Ben even thinking about them. The giant wave that had swept him out of the classroom seemed to be just behind him, however fast he went. He couldn't get away from it, and more importantly, he couldn't escape Mrs Craven, who, by the sound of the screams, was getting closer by the second.

Chapter 9   Help!

Everything had gone black. And
still. And silent. A strange, echoey
silence, as though any noise was a long,
long way away. Ben thought he was
probably dead. He decided he had
either been eaten by Mrs Craven, who
must have turned back into a giant sea
monster, or he had drowned in the huge
waves, or he had crashed into the wall
at the end of the corridor. Ben
wondered what his mum would say
when she found out. Probably say it
was all his own fault and he must have
been messing about as usual.
Something was lifting Ben. Up, up, up.

Out of the blackness. Out of the stillness. Away from the strange, echoey silence. Perhaps he wasn't dead, after all. Ben felt himself being hoisted out of the water by a pair of strong arms. The water made a loud sucking noise, and Ben emerged, spluttering and blinking, his legs hanging limply, like two pieces of cooked spaghetti.

Ben blinked open his eyes. He blinked again, trying to clear them, and found himself staring straight into a pair of thick black-rimmed glasses. The eyes behind them were hugely magnified, wide open and staring. Staring straight back at Ben, as though now *he* was some sort of strange sea monster. It was Mr McCann, and he was still halfway up the ladder. Only now the ladder was wobbling dangerously as Mr McCann struggled to hold Ben out of the water, *and* keep himself steady. Ben grabbed at the sides of the ladder and lowered himself carefully onto the nearest step. His whole body felt like jelly.

"What on earth – , " Mr McCann shouted, keeping one eye on Ben, and the other on the swirling water, "what on earth is going on?!"

Ben opened his mouth to answer,

although he wasn't at all sure what he was going to say. "I.....I....." he began, his teeth chattering, but the rest of the sentence was drowned out by the horrendous screaming that was getting closer and closer and louder and louder. Mr McCann turned his head and looked back over his shoulder. At the same time, something large and heavy crashed into the side of the step ladder, knocking its legs so hard that they skidded along the floor in the opposite direction to the platform at the top. Ben found himself being catapulted up in the air, alongside a very bemused looking Mr McCann. The last thing he noticed before flying through the office hatch and landing on Mrs Brookes' desk, was Mrs Craven, soaking wet and shaking, but hanging on desperately to one leg of the step ladder. So *that* was what had crashed into them, thought Ben, before collapsing on top of a pile of letters, informing parents that Mrs Craven took water safety *very* seriously and to *please* ensure your children remember their swimming kits *every* week.

Mrs Brookes, luckily, was nowhere to be seen. She got cross if you came to the hatch and asked a question without knocking. What she would do to a child flying through the hatch and landing on her desk in his swimming trunks was almost too much to bear thinking about. There was also no sign of Mr McCann. Ben decided he must have crashed into the wall beside the hatch. After all, there was no way Mr McCann could have flown through it like *he* had. Ben giggled to himself at the thought of Mr McCann getting stuck in the hatch, his top half in the office, his bottom half in the corridor, arms and legs waving in the air. Ben crawled on all fours across the desk, leaving a wet trail behind him, like a giant snail. He knelt up and peered through the hatch. The water had reached the front door and looked as though it was waiting to be let out. Ben watched, open mouthed, as Mr McCann heaved himself into an upright position and waded, against the tide, towards Mrs Craven. She had scrambled onto the fallen ladder and was now sitting cross-legged on top, as though onboard some home-made life raft. Her hair was stuck to her head, her glasses were nowhere to be seen, and one of her dangly earrings was hanging from a button on her blouse. In her left hand she held a metre rule, which looked as though it was about to become a makeshift oar. Ben wondered whether Mrs Craven knew that you wouldn't get far with just one oar. In fact, you would probably only go round in circles. Ben would have been quite happy for Mrs Craven to start rowing with the ruler. At least it would give him a chance to make his escape.

Chapter 10   <u>**No Time to Lose**</u>

Ben could hear voices. He guessed that Mr McCann had reached the stepladder. Ben bent towards the hatch and strained his ears, taking care not to be seen in the corridor.

"Mr McCann," Mrs Craven was saying in a shaky voice. She sounded angry, but controlled. Ben had heard that voice before, "I want to you to go straight up the corridor -". Ben thought he heard Mr McCann gasp. Or was it a sigh? Did Mrs Craven realise that the corridor was still full of water? Mrs Craven continued, "- and tell Mrs Peacock to *leave the building immediately.*" There was a short pause, "and *not to return*. Her wages will be in the post. *I* will teach her class from now on"

Now it was Ben's turn to gasp. Mrs Peacock, his favourite teacher. Going. And not returning. She had only filled the classroom with water to keep them quiet. He couldn't blame her. *And Mrs Craven teaching his class.* He had to act fast. Ben slid off the desk and crawled to the doorway. The coast was clear. Mr McCann had tied the stepladder to a door handle with piece of string. Mrs Craven was still sitting miserably on her liferaft, shivering, and staring up the corridor at Mr McCann's retreating back, as he made his way, half wading, half swimming, to Mrs Peacock's classroom.

Ben knew that he had to reach the classroom before Mr McCann did. There was only one way to do this. He would have to get there by going outside, climbing up the hosepipe, over the roof and down into the classroom. There was a door at the back of Mrs Brookes' office. That door led outside. There was no time to lose. By the time Ben had scooted along the side of the building and heaved himself up onto the roof, he could hardly breathe. He was freezing and panting heavily. He leaned over the skylight and looked down into the classroom. Somebody had managed to push the door shut after Ben had been swept out, but a lot of water had escaped with him. He was surprised to see the children standing on the floor, the water up to their shoulders. They were gathered in front of Mrs Peacock, who was looking thoughtful, as though she was trying to decide what to do next. Before she could do anything, Ben swung into action. "Who needs Superman underpants," he said to himself, as he grabbed the end of the hosepipe and jumped through the skylight, "I *am* Superman. Whhhheeeeee!!"

Ben shut his eyes and bent his knees. His body made a loud smacking sound as it hit the water, producing a huge spray which sent several children reeling backwards. Mrs Peacock wobbled, and opened her mouth wide, in astonishment, "B-B-Ben Bailey," she stuttered, "what are you doing back here?"

"I've come to rescue you," he said, looking straight back at Mrs Peacock. All eyes were on Ben. "Right," he said quickly, turning to his classmates, "we need to get Mrs Peacock up on top of the cupboard." Joe Rimmer burst out laughing. Mrs Peacock opened her mouth wide again, "What!" she exclaimed. "Mrs Peacock," said Ben, earnestly, "please. Just do it. You're in danger. Mrs Craven wants to get rid of you." Mrs Peacock's open mouth made a sort of squeaking noise.

"Jake, on my shoulders," said Ben, grabbing his friend's arm. Jake did as he was told. Ben glanced around him, peering through Jake's legs, "Now you, Joe, on Jake's shoulders, then Megan. Then - " He looked directly at Mrs Peacock, "Mrs Peacock, you need to climb up all of us, and onto the cupboard." Mrs Peacock nodded dumbly. She began to scramble up the human totem pole, as hands reached out to push and pull her to the top. She balanced for a few seconds on Megan's shoulders, before taking a deep breath, and with one last burst of energy, heaved herself up onto the cupboard. She slumped down onto a pile of books, sending them slithering across the top of the cupboard. Ben looked up proudly. It didn't really matter if she looked like a beached whale, it didn't matter that her hat had been dragged down over her eyebrows so that she could hardly see, it didn't even matter that her swirly pink and purple bottom was right now squashing Ben's model of a stegosaurus, made out of cereal boxes and aerosol tops. All that mattered was that Mrs Peacock was safe.

"Now listen everyone," Ben said importantly, and, taking a deep breath, began to explain his plan.

Chapter 11   <u>Rescue</u>

There was a loud splashing noise outside the classroom door, followed by a thump. Ben looked through the window at the top. Mr McCann had arrived. He looked exhausted and was resting his head against the door. Even from his position on the other side of the door, Ben could see that Mr McCann was taking a while to recover from his swim up the corridor. His eyes were squeezed shut and he was breathing very heavily. Ben looked round at his classmates. They were standing ready. They all knew exactly what they had to do. As the door began to slowly open,

Ben felt his stomach do a somersault of excitement. He was going to save Mrs Peacock if it was the last thing he did. Mr McCann pushed at the door with what little strength he had left after his swim. Water began to gush out, and Mr McCann waded in. He looked around the room in amazement, his eyes darting from child to child. Ben guessed he was looking for Mrs Peacock, and glanced up at the top of the cupboard. Mrs Peacock had rolled back towards the wall. All that could be seen were a few quivering flowers from her hat. His stegosaurus was well and truly gone now.

"Mrs Peacock?" Mr McCann said weakly, turning his head from side to side, "Mrs Peacock?" His eyes rested on Joe Rimmer. Joe looked at Ben. Ben stepped forward and jutted out his chin importantly, "Mrs Peacock isn't going anywhere." He said in a loud voice.

"Too right!" shouted Jake. Mr McCann glanced at him without expression and turned back to Ben, "Mrs Craven says - " he began, wearily, " – that Mrs Peacock is to leave the school immediately and not come back."

"*Booooooo!*" that was Joe Rimmer, good old Joe, thought Ben.

"*Mrs Craven - *" continued Mr McCann.

"*Boooooo!*"

"*Mrs Craven* will be teaching this class from now on." Said Mr McCann quickly, before there were any more interruptions.

"*Brooooooo!*" this time the whole class joined in, "*Booooo! Booooo!!*"

Ben raised his arms and waved his hands up and down until the booing stopped. It was like conducting an orchestra. He suddenly felt very important. Everybody was looking at him, waiting to hear what he had to say. "If Mrs Peacock leaves the school," he said firmly, "we all leave." A loud cheer went up. Ben grinned and conducted wildly again.

Before Mr McCann could reply, Ben added, "If Mrs Peacock stays, then we'll all be well-behaved and quiet. All the time. Every day. No need for water in the classroom. *And -* " he had just thought of this and he hoped this might do the trick, " *– and* we'll rescue Mrs Craven, *and* clear up all the mess."

He stared hard at Mr McCann, who stared back, looking very uncomfortable. Nobody spoke. After a minute, Mr McCann said, "I'll go and speak to Mrs Craven."

"*Yeah!*" shouted Jake, punching the air, and missing the back of Megan's head by millimetres.

The children watched as Mr McCann turned and waded out of the classroom. Ben could hear the splashing as he made his way down the corridor, back to where Mrs Craven was safely moored on her liferaft. The classroom was silent. All ears were listening to the low rumble of voices from the corridor. It seemed like a very long time before Mr McCann returned, red-faced and sweating. He stood for a minute, breathing heavily and wiping his brow with the back of his hand. Eventually he said, "Mrs Craven - " he paused to rub at his chest with the palm of his hand. Ben held his breath.

"Mrs Craven says that if you let all the water out of the classroom......,"

Ben nodded.

"And get every last drop of water out of school......,"

Ben nodded again.

"And clean up all the mess......,"

Everybody was nodding now.

"And get Mrs Craven off the stepladders and back into her office......,"

Jake and Amy looked at each other and frowned. Ben nodded. He was the only one who knew that Mrs Craven was stuck on some stepladders tied to a door handle down the corridor. He would explain later to the rest of the class. For now he wanted to know whether Mrs Peacock could stay.

"Yes?" he said to Mr McCann, willing him to say what they all wanted to hear. "Then.....," said Mr McCann, his face breaking into a smile, "then......."

"*What?*" shouted Ben. Mr McCann was teasing them now, with all these "thens".

"Then Mrs Peacock can stay." A loud cheer rose up, filling the classroom. Water began to bubble as the children jumped up and down, punching the air and lunging at each other in delight. Ben grinned from ear to ear. They'd done it. *He'd* done it. He'd saved Mrs

Peacock. Mr McCann clamped his hands to his ears, screwed up his eyes and turned towards the door. A quivering pink flower moved slowly along the top of the cupboard.

Chapter 12   <u>All Change Back</u>

Ben didn't really know where to start. He had only thought about saving Mrs Peacock, he hadn't thought about what he would do once he had saved her. He looked around the room helplessly. The others were just messing about, whooping and shouting and giving each other high fives. He needed to get things in order. And quickly. Otherwise, as sure as eggs is eggs, as his grandma would say, Mrs Peacock would go, and Mrs Craven would be in, teaching his class. No more magic conkers, no more carrots with legs, no more puppets that came to life, no more eating fruit in the playground, just nine to three boredom. Ben wondered what his mum would do in this situation. He thought about all the times the house had been a mess (caused by him and Ella) and how his mum got busy, and before you knew it, everything was back to how it should be. Usually just before his dad walked through the door. He pictured his mum, busy with the hoover, throwing toys back in the box, ticking things off a list.

A list, that was it. He needed to make a list. His mum always said if you had a list you could do anything – and tick it off as you did it. That way, you could see what you still needed to do. She had tried to make Ben do lists for his homework projects, but he could never be bothered. He never got beyond, "write name and date at top of paper". It was a waste of time. But now, suddenly, he could see the point of it. They would make a list and tick things off as they did them. Ben turned to face the whiteboard. The water level had dropped and there was enough room to make a list on the board. A red pen hung from a lump of blu-tack above the board. Ben hoped it would still work after being submerged in water. He grabbed the pen and turned back to his classmates.

"Right!" he shouted, sounding just like Mrs Peacock. The others stopped messing and looked at Ben, expectantly. "We've got a lot to do if we want to keep Mrs Peacock," he said, glancing up at the top of the cupboard. The flowers on the hat shook. "First we need to make a list."

"That's a good idea," said Joe Rimmer, much to Ben's surprise. He smiled back at Joe.

"OK, you lot shout out and I'll write it on the whiteboard."

Within a few minutes, Ben had written his list. He wasn't too sure of all the spellings but he didn't think Mrs

Peacock would mind, just for once. It was all in a good cause. There were ten items on the list. Ten things to do before home time. He read it through quickly to himself.

1. get worter out of classroom

2. get larst drop of worter out of school

3. get mrs cravan of ladders

4. get mrs cravan into her offis

5. dry mrs cravans cloths (Ben wasn't too sure how they were going to do this, and he didn't really like to think about it too much. He hoped she would have some ideas herself).

6. dry books that are wet

7. evrybody get chaingd

8. hang swiming things on pegs

9. put desks back in rihgt plases

10. make shor evrything is reddy
for munday

Ben let out his breath in a long sigh, "Is that everything?" he asked the others. "What about Mrs Peacock?" said Megan, worriedly, "we can't leave her up there." She nodded her head towards the top of the cupboard. The flowers wobbled and shook. Ben couldn't believe he'd forgotten about Mrs Peacock in all this. He turned back to the board. "11," He wrote quickly, "get mrs peecok of the cubbard."

Ben decided that he and Jake should rescue Mrs Craven. Maybe he wouldn't feel so bad then for locking her in her office earlier that day. It seemed a long time ago now. A lot had happened since then. Ben opened the door, and once again, was swept along on a tide of water. Jake was right behind him, arm and legs waving in the air. Ben could see Mrs Craven bobbing up and down on the ladders as the swell of water hit them. She watched anxiously as Ben and Jake were tossed towards her.

"Grab the ladders!" shouted Ben to Jake, reaching out his right arm towards them. Jake lunged towards the ladders and grabbed at a step. Mrs Craven wobbled back and forth for a few seconds before steadying herself. She smiled for the first time that morning, "Thank you boys," she said, "thank you so much. You must each have a sticker for your charts for this kind act." Ben didn't have the heart to tell her the sticker charts were floating soggily about the classroom, and most of the stickers had come unstuck anyway. "Do you know," continued Mrs Craven, as Ben and Jake untied the string and began to guide the ladders towards Mrs Craven's office, "*somebody -* " she paused to convey her shock, "*somebody locked me in my office this morning."* Ben and Jake concentrated on the ladders. Ben didn't dare look at Jake. "Anyway, you two have restored my faith in human nature." Mrs Craven nodded and smiled at the two boys. Ben hadn't got a clue what she was talking about, but he guessed it was good as she looked happy and she wasn't telling them off. Thank goodness she didn't know it had been Ben who had turned that key.

The boys steered the ladders into Mrs Craven's office, past Mrs Brookes, who was sitting on her desk with her head in her hands. The newsletters floated about the room. "Thank you again, boys," said Mrs Craven, "as soon as the water's gone I shall get off these ladders and change into my PE kit." Ben stifled a giggle. He couldn't imagine Mrs Craven in PE kit. It would be even worse that Mrs Peacock in that swirly pink and purple swimming costume. Jake followed Ben out of Mrs Craven's office and back past Mrs Brookes. The water level had dropped dramatically and was nearly down to the floor. Newsletters were stuck along the walls. There was one stuck to Mrs Brookes' back. Ben guessed she didn't know or she would have removed it. She always liked to look so perfect. A

107

newsletter on your back wasn't exactly the height of fashion, even Ben knew that.

The boys didn't have to swim back up the corridor. The water was gushing out of the front door and cascading down the path, sending little rivulets across the playground. Ben thought it was like wading through a deep puddle on the way back, the sort that his mum made him put his wellies on for. She'd get a shock if she could see him now, he thought, grinning to himself and kicking the water before him.

Numbers one, six, seven, eight and nine had been ticked off the list by the time Ben and Jake returned to the classroom.

"Well done everyone," said Ben, proudly, looking round the room at the books steaming on the radiators and the desks back in their neat groups. The floor was still wet but there wasn't even enough for a puddle in here. Everybody had changed back into school uniform, although they were still rather damp looking, and swimming things had been hung on pegs. Ben reached for the pen and ticked off numbers four and five, even though Mrs Craven's dry clothes weren't quite a definite yet. He was sure they soon would be. This was going well.

"Jake and I need to get changed now," said Ben, "then all we need to do is make sure there isn't a drop of water left in school and everything's ready for Monday," he grinned round at everyone, "and then we'll get Mrs Peacock down."

They decided it might be best if they passed Mrs Peacock's towel and clothes up to her, on top of the cupboard, where she could get dressed without getting wet again. They would dry the floor, check the corridor, make sure Mrs Craven was happy, and then they would get Mrs Peacock down. For now, thought Ben, she's safer up there.

By the time the bell rang at 3 O'clock, Ben felt as though he had done a week's work. Class 4P spilled out of school and headed for home. On Fridays Ben's mum always picked him up. They went shopping, which he hated, although it wasn't so bad if Jake and his mum came too. It looked as though that was the plan tonight. The two mums were deep in conversation, nodding and laughing. Ben's mum absently rocked the pram as she talked. Ben and Jake zigzagged across the playground, towards them.

"How was your swimming?"

asked Ben's mum, taking his bag and putting it under the buggy. "Fine," said Ben, looking at Jake. Jake grinned. "Still don't know what that nutty woman's playing at," said Ben's mum, half to Ben and half to Jake's mum, "she needs to make her mind up, that one." Jake's mum laughed and shook her head.

"Oh, she has," said Ben, grinning back at Jake, "she definitely has. No more swimming on a Friday. She said she thinks we'll stick to once a week in future."

22087496R00063

Printed in Great Britain
by Amazon